OBLIVION

J. Rod

Oblivion
J. Rod

First edition December 2021
First published Mexico City, March 2021

Index

Oblivion is an act of self—love. It is looking in the mirror and realizing that the most important person in the world is that reflection with strengths and weaknesses. It is looking for a forceful alternative to eliminate physical and mental pain and be happy. Forgetfulness occurs in any person, place or in any dimension. This story is one of forgetfulness, without names of people, places, or references. It is about one more life in any remote part of the universe trying to forget in order to be able to love himself again. And perhaps, if hope never dies, love again the only person in the world who can achieve happiness, even if it depends on third parties and innumerable complex factors to converge positively. Only love can do it. Even if it is a leap into the void, only a brave person or a dreamer would do it.

First part

I thought I had forgotten the silk of her skin forever, but I was walking through an informal path formed by lush rose bushes when I realized my gross mistake. A branch pried with the force of my arm and a stream of thorns grated my back causing me immense pain, followed by a rose crashing on my face, releasing soft petals that touched my cheeks and my chin. The scratches of the thorns were less painful than the tears running down my eyes, because on a spring night I saw her silhouette disappear walking on a street of unfortunate memories. It was so strange to feel her again in the smoothness of the petals of that rose, that my mind quickly evoked countless images, one after another, of the moments with her. If I had avoided that thorny path, my body would not be shuddering at every sensation brought on by remembering her lips on mine. And even more so, when that smoothness was only compared to the softness of her cheeks or her crotch. I knew it perfectly; I had been hundreds of times in that place. I walked home. The aromas of the vegetation, in that beautiful park, made me smile permanently.

For a moment, I did not want to get away from there; however, I could not continue to be enchanted and suffer again for not having her. The edge of the park was an abrupt blow back to reality: immediately, the smell of burning fuel, cigarettes and asphalt, coupled with the bustle of car engines, voices and the crash of shoes on the floor of the cars pedestrians, everything returned to a very empty normality.

Once again, I was alone in the world, among billions of people circulating daily near my life. Sometimes so close hitting my chest accidentally from the immense traffic and my carelessness when walking. Sometimes I have even been insulted for my clumsiness when walking. Sometimes also some people have accidentally burned my arm with the tip of their cigar when hitting me. That is my daily routine: walking from the appearance of the first rays of the sun burning my eyelashes until the moment when the night totally covers the sky. I walk from end to end of the island, passing by the seashore until crossing some buildings, and returning to the other limit of this small piece of land.

I get drunk on the grail of the breeze to try not to think of anything else. I watch the blue horizon come to an end with the sky and the setting sun. I listen to music to relax and drink the traditional peanut liquor and have even tried, without success, to touch someone else, but have not been successful. I have practiced that routine of keeping all my senses occupied so that I can keep my nose away from the aroma of perfume combined with her sweat, trick my taste buds with strong flavors to dissolve the delicious poison inoculated by her lips on mine. Mesmerize my mind fixing my eyes on the most beautiful sunset landscapes.

Devour the violent beats of the bass and drums to stun me with the music at great decibels so as not to hear her voice, which reaches my ears every day on the island. On several occasions I have kissed other lips and the skin of other women until I was inches from reaching the bottom of her body, but at that moment hers appears in my thoughts and the pleasure, satisfaction and hope end. That is why I chose, the last month, only to dedicate myself to four senses; leave aside the carnal part and go deeper, what had entered my mind, apparently, never to leave. And yet, the day I was sure I could be with someone else, that heinous accident happened. The softness of the petals unearthed all the memories of her in my mind, in a noisy way. And my personal therapy in this place went through that channel that leads to the sea to get lost and never return. I thought that I had no reason to continue in this place, wherever I went, her shadow would chase me everywhere.

Annoyed, I packed my bags and prepared to return to the nearest city, the one on the coast, where I was born and met her.

I set sail on an ancient ship. The crossing was longer, but I had time to meditate for hours with my gaze lost in the immensity of the sea. For moments, I was afraid to return to the place where I was born, where she arrived years later. I should not have left; it was my home. Seven years I had spent in exile, and probably no one remembered me anymore. I left when I was from the generation of the twenties, those who live on dreams and illusions, who believe in eternal love, like mine towards her, and I returned in the thirties, when maturity begins to sprout, to understand to blows that nothing and nobody is forever. When you learn from the mistakes of youth and to be stronger.

The sea has always been my fascination, in any latitude or tone of the millions that are formed on the continents by the variety of rocks, plants and components formed over centuries. For this reason, traveling in that ancient boat evoked the stories of those centuries, when a knight went in search of his fiancée. This time I just longed for peace and quiet. Determined to start over, loneliness was perhaps an advantage. Not having a loved one in the world made a sedentary life in search of happiness easier. I was hoping to return to my city. I should have not run anywhere else, even if the possibility of accidentally finding her was always latent, but this time I decided to face her and overcome her.

My city was still an immense town, where they still went out to drink coffee on the terraces of their houses, while they felt the sea breeze and greeted each other even without knowing each other. They had not become addicted to mobile devices. Sometimes there was no signal and it went unnoticed by the villagers. But, for me, the internet was moderately important, to be able to supervise the businesses that I inherited from my parents. I was fortunate to have had two successful professionals at home.

I rented a room in a hotel near the beach, which seemed like a run—of—the—mill hotel, however, I had an ideal space to put my passion into practice: gardening. I always wanted to plant the roses that would one day adorn my balcony and hers, and now I had the time to do so.

The first month I only went out to the streets to buy the necessary supplies to plant, and spent hours playing among the earth to be the creator of a beautiful garden, completely dirtying my hands and clothes, wearing my hands to feel like someone useful. I imagined that all that effort, in a couple of years, would change the appearance of the place. There I could lie down in a hammock to feel the gentle breeze from the sea, while drinking hot coffee in the winter and ice—cold beer in the summer.

At least I was able to smile several times envisioning myself in the future. I imagined her happy forming a family and I was just a simple spectator.

For an instant I managed to let out that pride that I had lost after she left, and I thought to myself:

"I was not born the day I met you,

Before you, my world had already revolved many times around the sun,

My eyes had already observed the wonders of the planet.

Before you, I was already great,

And since I was, I can be countless times.

And if one day I found you by chance I am sure,

You will be sadder to have lost me,

Than me if I wasn't the one who took you to the aisle".

I was bragging, exaggeratedly, when the icy water from the water dispenser installed in the garden began to soak my shirt and I ran inside. Not even being alone did she stop overwhelming me. When I tried to minimize it, destiny would appear and slap me, like that wet one that, coupled with the humid weather and the low temperature of that afternoon, caused me a bad cold and to stay in bed for a couple of days drinking all kinds of infusions.

In a month, a green fortress was almost built. Beautiful plants and flowers would grow all around the house, and according to my calculations some vines would reach the roof. Plants were my passion, like animals for many other people, except that my love for plants was not only aesthetic or emotional, but also scientific, since they purify the air, they are living beings, they enrich the soil, they provide shade and many other benefits. The best company of man, for me, was not an animal. Whoever said that was more wrong than vegans, who do not eat meat so as not to hurt animals. In that case we should not do it with plants either because they are more essential, they also have life and feel. Bah! Radical thoughts business.

Summer was beginning and temperatures above forty degrees made it necessary to go out to take the sea breeze, to stop feeling the body boiling by the merciless rays of the sun. It was a balm to spend the whole day lying on the sand, I felt relaxed but a little dehydrated. Surely the next day I would feel the ravages of being exposed to the sun on my skin, which did not worry me, since I had many natural remedies at home to mitigate the damage. Let the whites worry, because their skin burns and wrinkles faster, but for dark ones or dark ones like me, that was a light caress.

I loved all that life around the beach. I spent a large part of my youth there. There was still the palapa where we all arrived in the afternoons, after leaving university, to admire the waves and chat like great friends. I was draining in sweat and I craved a craft beer, made in the place so much that it alluded to the mythical God Quetzalcoatl. I sat at the bar of seats made of oak logs and covered with coconut palm. I ordered the largest jar and drank it like water to hydrate myself and start the walk home. I felt a relief when that delicious drink ran through my body and at the same time the cool breeze blew my face. I got up satisfied leaving the money from the account on the bar and started my way out of that historic place, at least for me. The rays of the sun seemed weak compared to that intense light hitting my pupils, although it was only an instant, not even fixed, but it was reason to feel tiny in the world I always wanted to live. I was audacious to think that she would recognize me at the first moment, as if I were someone who attracted attention. I was an idiot to think of her gaze fixing on mine, as if my extra pounds, gray hair and hair loss over the years were quick to identify. I, too, could barely recognize her. I stood in front of her table surrounded by several friends so that she could identify me. I thought I would be more distant, colder, I thought of being disappointed in her by not feeling the same as I did seven years ago.

I was still shocked to find her there, especially since she was married, and probably with a nice family to live with and not having fun in these places for young people or abandoned singles like me. She immediately got up from the chair, went to greet me effusively and begin to say goodbye to her friends, since she apparently had another commitment. With every step that she approached me; my heart began to beat with a speed never seen before.

— Years without knowing anything about you, you disappeared from the face of the earth, — she told me, and I just nodded. I did not know what to say: I was too nervous to have her in front of me, her right hand resting on my chest. — Look, I must go. My husband is waiting for me at home.

Her words were like a dagger stuck in my chest: that night she would sleep hugging him and I in a corner of my bed.

— But on another occasion that we coincide, you tell me what has happened to your life in these years and we catch up. Ok? — she told me to get me out of my sad reflections.

— Okay. Take care of yourself, nice night, —I replied like an automaton. I could not think of anything and less express something. I said goodbye to her and when she was going to leave the place, she turned to see me, and came back, she winked at me smiling and sweetly released me:

—Do not! I cannot wait until I find you again to hear from you. So, let us sit down for fifteen minutes so you can tell me something.

Immediately, she took me by the hand and led us to an empty table for two, right next to the table where her friends were still, which seemed logical to me: a married woman should not arouse suspicion.

I thought about just spending a few nice minutes with her and closing that circle, but damn it! I saw her more beautiful than ever and I wish it was only her beauty, her gaze made me inexplicably weak, like that time when her smile made me never yearn for anything other than kissing her. I thought that when I saw her again, I could highlight her defects and take her away from my thoughts, but the only thing that I took away from my head was the world, because I only concentrated on her and the indescribably immense desire to hug her and squeeze her tight, because no longer just her gaze mesmerized me and her smile sweetened me, but it suffocated me to see her legs and her delicate body so close. I do not know if I was right or wrong in agreeing to sit down with her to talk that day, I just know that I realized that I could never forget her.

— What happen? Are you very distracted? Does something bother you? - She, she asked me.

What if something bothered me? I answered myself. Of course, I do, it bothers me that you do not live with me. No doubt she noticed my clumsiness as I spilled some of the beer, I had asked for to chat for a few moments. My lack of concentration was derived from her penetrating gaze upon my eyes. She looked confident, and I wavered at every moment, intimidated by her imposing presence. She was the owner of time and space.

—It's nothing, I was just very surprised to find you, — I barely managed to tell her with shaking hands playing with the saltshaker on the table.

— In my opinion, I have not heard from you in almost a decade, tell me: where have you been? Do you still live in the city? Did you get married? Do you have children? Do you continue with the consulting business?

Her interest made me feel important, but so many questions collapsed my mind, and I did not know what to say. She drank some of a martini that she had ordered when we first sat down at the table and I remembered when those lips touched every part of my skin, without any shame.

—I went to live on the island, — I told her, and she looked at me strangely. I live alone, I have not married, and I have no children.

I lacked the courage to tell her that I only wanted to have children with her. And in my fantasy, I thought that she felt the same because for the first time I saw her safety knocked down and she also hesitated to put her glass on the table when my eyes penetrated her pupils.

— To the island? I cannot believe it! That place is not to live — she told me joking —. Who can be happy in that place?

And she was right: I was not happy there, but at least I did not suffer that excruciating fire for not having her.

—I wanted to try something different, new airs, — I replied as I took a long drink of the craft beer, without stopping for a single moment seeing her lips moistened by her drink. I did not know when I would see them again, so I had to take advantage.

— Something different? You better have committed a crime and gone to jail. You would be in a much better place than the island.

Her jokes stole a laugh from me, as nobody did in years.

— The island has its own thing. It is a good place to meditate and reflect. There I got rid of all my problems.

— And what problems did you want to release? — she questioned me.

Faced with such a question, I should have answered: —you. You really have been my adorable problem all this time. — But I did not have the guts, again, to tell her what was eating me.

— Unimportant things, better tell me how you are doing in your married life? — I chose to answer her.

Before answering me, she looked at her watch, worried, surely, she should go see her husband or take, if she had them, her children to some sporting or artistic engagement in the afternoon. It was the weekend and she probably had a lot more options than sitting with me in a bar.

— It is an exceptionally long story, that's why I told you a while ago that only fifteen minutes would not be enough for us to talk. We have many details to tell. So, we will have to schedule ourselves for next week and tell you at length.

She kept her keys and asked for her bill, but I refused to let her pay, so she took her things and she only managed to summarize seven years for me in almost the same number of words:

— My married life is going very well — she said with a smile that far from pleasing me buried me — The only new thing is that he is not the same person you met.

At that moment I felt how all the strength in my body was fading, and she came over to kiss me on the cheek and say goodbye.

—You were right, that guy was disgusting so I divorced him at eleven months, but a year ago I remarried, and my life feels much happier and more peaceful. I hope you can meet him now that you are living here again.

For my part, I just nodded my head automatically and I raised my hand in goodbye as she walked away until she was lost through the exit door of the place.

— Sir! Sir! Excuse me, is something wrong? — I barely listened to the waiter of the place worried because I was immobile and with a lost look. My whole body was weighed against the seat.

—No, thanks, — I said with my voice broken by the lump in my throat after that revelation. I could barely speak— Bring me the bill please.

Second part

I walked many blocks thinking incessantly about her. At every step I felt that the depth of her gaze and her immense smile stunned me until I was walking almost unconscious through the streets of that city, which now seemed unknown to me. I traveled all the corners of the place where she lived, while I thought about her repeatedly. For moments, I felt the most immense joy of having seen her smile once more, but I was also trapped by the nostalgia and sadness of thinking that I could have made that smile mine forever and undo it with a kiss whenever I wanted. Sometimes it was courage that invaded the torrent of my blood that flowed as I passed through the places that I could have shared with her: in the rain, sun or cold, filling with happiness the deserted streets that I was traveling at that time, and how explain what I felt when I passed by that church, the one we once imagined would be ours. I felt like crying at the thought that this could be the beginning of a story that will never be. Sometimes it also crossed my mind that, if I had the opportunity to turn back time, it would be to walk around here as I should have done years before. And not having waited for everything to be impossible, and maybe that is why I did it unconsciously. I do not know. Maybe I was afraid that the doubt seen in her eyes, when I met her, would be the same as now. For that reason, perhaps, I did not have the courage to look for her, and for fear that what I inexplicably felt that time for her was not the same.

And it is that I have never explained myself, as much as I have tried to understand it, how can someone fall in love with another person from the first day of meeting them and never forget them? It sounds ridiculous, but I could not explain it because her presence attracted me from the moment I saw her for the first time. I could not explain how in a dark place and surrounded by so many people I could appreciate each of her features. It sounds as unreal as thinking that I would have met her in another life. Otherwise, it sounds so inexplicable and even silly of me to fall in love in an instant. But that is how it was, and that is why I lived the happiest years of my life when we were together. And maybe for that reason I felt stupid, to think that she felt the same thing that I felt one day, or maybe I just protected myself. At times, with the cold night, I adopted the attitude of feeling calm for not having been here when I was able to win her back, making her feel the same as when she stole all my senses and I was a faithful slave of her will, but immediately she smiled again telling myself that that was just a pretext for my stupidity, to justify myself for having lost her, or rather for having lost the opportunity to conquer the world that exists behind her eyes. I gave up, in exile, before I could fight, and that frustrated me at every corner I passed, which became nothing when I remembered her again in that white dress and the nerves I felt before seeing her get up from that table bar, after having traveled miles to try to forget her.

***

That Saturday the chronicle of an announced death was consummated, so it was published in the newspapers. It was rumored in the corridors of the most elegant coffee shops in the city, it was spread by our mutual friends on their social networks. The locals replicated it in every corner of the city as the most bombastic social engagement of the year. Every minute that passed was one more nail in my coffin, and yet I waited until the last moment. I parked a block from the church and stood there, helpless, like a dying onlooker, watching the love of my life get out

17

of a vehicle adorned with white bows to head for the entrance. Every step from her to the altar was a gunshot wound opening my heart. Dying, I got out of my car and entered the church decorated in every corner in detail. I tried to go unnoticed to sit on the last bench. It was the farthest place in the event. I could not be left with the doubt until that moment when I heard from her lips: yes I accept.

I died the day I lost her and died again seven years later, but no longer at the door of a church, but at a bar table.

I got to the house and went straight to the garden. That loneliness could reassure me. I was hitting walls everywhere. Each blow was to an image of her ex—husband, the next to her new husband, which I still did not know, and the third to my face for having been so delusional. I approached the rose bush, my favorite because each petal reminds me of the texture of her skin, and with each hand I tightly squeezed a branch from each end, with all the anger pouring out of me I tried to pull so hard until I pulled out the entire rose bush, but I could not. With my bleeding hands pierced by thorns and my face flooded with tears, I sobbed and looked at the beauty of those flowers. I could not do it. The beautiful roses in my garden could not afford my ineptitude. Thousands of times I screamed: —Why was this happening to me? — So, I spent the whole afternoon squeezing the soil in the garden to vent. The rain painted the scene even more tragic: muddy, back to the mud, cold drops fell on my face and together with my tears covered all visibility. I stayed there sobbing until my tired body was exhausted.

I woke up to the noise of birdsong, lying in the garden, full of dried mud on my body and clothes, looking up at the blue sunny sky of dawn. My whole body ached, and my face was swollen from crying. I made some coffee and the first thing I did before breakfast was take the only suitcase I had out of the closet. I shuffled around the room putting my belongings away. My body, cold from the rain, could barely smell the unpleasant mud. I did not want to stay a fraction of a second longer in my city, the one where I was born and died in life.

I waited there in the port leaning on a cold bench until I got a ticket to the island. Again, I returned defeated and with the same trunk of memories, without treasuring more pleasant moments in my life, only gall. That moment passed through my mind six years ago when I should have been here and not now, to alleviate the pain of separation and have the most important opportunity of my life: to get her back, but very cowardly I was hidden in a span of land of the island.

They were heavy hours for my mind during the journey. The road back to exile is usually harder a second time. It is a couple of accumulated losses, dying twice, it's inexplicably painful. In the first it was to bleed me completely until I stopped breathing. In the second, no longer heartbeat, it was simply losing the last probable signs of life in my body. And so, dead alive, I reached the shore of the island again just as it was dawn. Although the sky looked clear and beautiful, the day was dark.

Nothing had changed in the short time of my absence. The few streets of the center crowded with people living together or buying, on the shores only sand and sea, the perfect medicine to forget, although still ineffective with me. On more than one occasion I thought of the simplest way out, walking out to sea until I got lost. But why take my life, if my heartbeat was hardly heard anymore, I was just breathing. I was one more inert object in the world, a painting of a tragedy or a sculpture of a debacle, in the middle of the living room of the house, constantly reminding me of my defeat. My life was, before my departure, very empty, trying to survive and overcome her. Now I did not even care about that, I only ate and drank when my body demanded it.

Every day I woke up when the sun's rays burned my face, almost at noon. There were times when I did not want to get out of bed, I just wanted to stay like that, immobile, just get up to go to the bathroom and come back, unconscious so as not to suffer anymore.

Sometimes in my dreams she would appear and thank God, most of the time, they were pleasant images and perhaps they were the only thing that colored my life and kept me beating.

I got back to my routine of walking all over the island, the first two weeks. Those closest to the event were the most difficult, later it became a habit, perhaps meaningless, but in the end it was a way to occupy my life.

I was walking along the west coast of the island again, with that beautiful sunny landscape shining in the sea, my bare feet were delighting in the softness of the sand, when one of the fishermen interrupted me. There were few in that area of the island, most of them were located on the eastern side, where the fruits of their labor paid off, and that is why I liked going there. In the first place, because in that part the rocks formed a pleasant sight when hitting the waves. Secondly, because it was a very relaxed and quiet space, and, thirdly, because of the confidence generated because I could almost recognize each of the men who were dedicated to fishing and because of my daily trips to that place.

He was perhaps the least pleasant for me because he was the youngest and most daring. On more than one occasion I had to see him throw his nets on the shore and leave his work lying around. Like most of his generation, he seemed to disdain work and even more so the family trade. On another occasion, he even made a gesture of almost vomiting from the smell of the breeze with the fish in the nets. I also felt disgusted, but because of his behavior, how disgusted he was going to feel about his daily work.

As I walked towards the sea, where I placed a rose among the waves every day in honor of her, he slapped my arm in disdain for being right in the way of his launch. I felt part of his web scrape off him with my arm and the smell of that youth cologne used by him to try to distinguish himself from others, as if a lotion were a source of education and elegance. Although he could not do it with great force, his tiny body compared to mine was like the flapping of a butterfly and yet it caused a tsunami in me. He bothered me so much, more because of his attitude of indifference, that, because of that touch, but his words were even more exhausting:

—Dude, don't you have something more important to do in your life than to come here to the shore to cry every day? —

It angered me that he realized how many times I had shed a couple of tears in front of the ocean. It bothered me even more to be so obvious to any stranger. The latter I do not know if he screamed it when he was already in her boat entering the ocean, or it was the product of my imagination accelerated at that moment by courage.

—You are right in everything you think, I suffer for working in something that I do not like, but you suffer for pleasure.

I was stunned by the words of that stranger, more than a daring he seemed an angel in the street opening a world of possibilities not visualized by my alienated mind.

His words penetrated the depths of my pride, but also of my still slightly latent hope. Even if his claims were only cruel to mock me, he was right in every argument. So, I thanked in my mind his advice or insult from him not asked for and returned to the house.

I leaned back on the most comfortable chair and drank some coffee. I had only two options: maintain the status quo and continue crying daily on the shore of the island or run to pack and leave the island for good. It was after the third long sip of coffee that I made my decision, and I even felt an idiot for not having decided at the same moment about the allegories of that insolent, even if I did not think his way of expressing myself, with all the annoyance I must have drop everything instantly and run to the city again, even without a shred of luggage, I just had to hurry to be on the other side of the river that separated me from her.

I decided to take the first outgoing boat, luckily at midnight I found a ticket. I was not worried about anything else. Fortunately, any slope could be solved remotely thanks to the new existing technologies. I was berating myself for going back to the island instead of staying in town and wasting time. On the other hand, I blessed the island because probably if I had not returned and reflected in exile, I would not have made the decision to return. It was a desperation to travel an hour in the dark of the night wishing every moment to see the lights of the city in the distance. When I noticed on my watch the minutes remaining to reach the destination port, I began to feel a tingling in my body and my chest to inflate to the point of exploding with excitement. It was like dynamite exploding on me. I went out to take a breath on the mast, to feel the breeze intoxicated with other aromas as a sign of being close to the shore. The smell of fresh fish and the early morning breeze in the markets near the port, far from displeasing me, brought back thousands of memories, it was my home, my home.

I was feeling very tired physically and emotionally. My home was close, so I decided to walk as soon as I got off the boat. It was difficult to enter my parents' old house, it brought me so many beautiful memories with them, of when I never felt fear or worry about anything because they were always there, relieving any pain and solving my problems. Sometimes I missed those moments too much. Just seeing that old cedar furniture room, now moldy from disuse, my jaw wobbled from side to side sobbing slightly and dripping a couple of tears. She and I were there on countless occasions, talking, debating, watching a movie and making love when everyone was asleep. I left the suitcase, unopened, at the entrance; I just wanted to get to a bed and rest to be one hundred percent early the next day, call her to finish the conversation that we did not finish weeks before.

Very early I began to make all the earrings, I arranged my things from the suitcase in my drawers, I shaved my beard from weeks, I cleaned a part of the house, I bought something for breakfast and I sat in my father's study to write one and again what I would say to her when having her in front of me, the indications of the precise moment, when she was concentrated listening to me, without possible distraction, perhaps even to boldly ask her to turn off her mobile phone, and beg the waiter no one to approach the table at the moment to see my signal. With the complicity of the owners of the local cafeteria, which I used to frequent when I lived here, they could put in the background the song that we chose as a waltz when we got married and that we never danced.

I called her at noon to try not to wake her up in the morning or at night and put her husband on alert. I was eager to hear her and nervous at the same time; I was prepared to see her the moment she told me, I was excited to think that like on that day, she immediately sat down with me to tell me about her life, in the same way when I marked her, she immediately told me to meet that same day. That was my expectation.

—I thought you would not call, — she told me with a slight voice of claim that I liked and made me feel important in her life.

—You were right in what you told me the other night: we must catch up and talk long and hard, — I replied and immediately came a couple of seconds of silence that terrified me thinking that she would reject my proposal.

—Mmm. — Look, this week I am going out of town to a wedding with my husband— I knew she was too beautiful to be real. I immediately thought that it was just a pretext to avoid me and it was logical: she was a married woman, and she was always clear about her principles —. But what do you think if next Monday, which is dinner day with my friends, I cancel them and you and I go to the cafeteria where you spilled my coffee on our first date?

OMG! How could she remember that and even more say it without feeling that choking in her throat that I felt when I heard it? That was precisely our first date and my nerves were such that my hands trembling from wanting to bring her sugar clumsily, I threw the cup on her dress, burning part of her legs. I felt so sorry that occasion that I thought I would never get a second chance with her.

— Are you available that day? — she pulled me out of my thoughts.

—Of course, you tell me what time and I will be there, — I said. My voice denoted the emotion of having managed to at least see her one more time. And now it was up to me to get it back or not.

The passing of the days was eternal: the hands of the clock moved very slowly; I could almost swear that every second was minutes. While waiting in the garden of the house, I wrote down each word step by step in a notebook: what I would say to her, crossed out and rewrote to find the right phrases, the ones that could reach the bottom of her heart and her mind. The complicated situation necessarily required not only the intervention of the heart to decide, but its way of reasoning my words and the morally difficult situation.

How would the most important speech of my life begin?

And that is how I took care of every word and finished writing at dawn. I read it several times to be sure not to forget any important detail, but above all trying to convey that I needed her to be happy.

Each day helped me to perfect my words and practice the moment, as well as to put the house in order. I was determined to stay here for the rest of my life.

The deadline was met. I woke up before the first rays of the sun appeared. I felt sure of myself for the first time in years. I took a few minutes to watch the sunrise on the horizon over the sea, while sipping some coffee before preparing for the most important appointment of my days. I sprayed all over my body with the lotion that she chose for me and with which one day I promised I would use only when I went to see her. When she told me, years ago, I thought it was crazy of her part, but then she became part of my routine too.

I went over the lines of my speech one by one, while I relaxed in the hammock located in the center of the garden of that old house of my parents. Up to there I could feel the breeze and it mitigated a little that tickling running through my entire body through the nerves of directly throwing all the love stored in my heart at it. A dark green jacket was my choice. Green was always her favorite color, and a plain dark tie complemented the outfit for the occasion. I arrived an hour early so I could relax with some tea. Fortunately, the place had a long list of infusions of all kinds, among which there were relaxants that I combined to calm me down and focus on achieving my goal. I went through the script a couple of times and how I should express each word so that it would not be misunderstood. The table was set.

Third part

Her entrance to the cafeteria was like every place she appeared: unparalleled, dazzling. She is the owner of my neurons, my guts, my time and space. She knew how to appropriate the attention of her own and strangers, generating envy and admiration among women, and catalyzing the most touching and perverted desires of men. That is how she was, she never went unnoticed. And it was not only in her physical beauty that her fine features, her sculpture, could be appreciated, but it was also her personality, the way she walked, with an enviable security for any woman and man in the world. Her smile, from her little lips, radiated immense joy. She took care of every detail of her clothing. With glasses, she used to hide her honey—colored eyes that made her more beautiful when they discovered them. She wore a perfume, which was perfection combined with the subtle sweat on her body, especially her neck. Her legs were part of that great appeal: thick from birth and perfectly shaped by the exercise carried out in the daily practice of her favorite sport, volleyball. Her voice was serious, she was imposed in any conversation, but delicate. The intelligence she possessed was extraordinary. Anyone could fall in love with her, listening to her for a couple of minutes, for her knowledge of any subject of hers, excellent sense of humor and relaxing rhythm of her voice.

This is how I fell in love with her, at the beginning of spring, when we were both just twenty years old, when I saw her enter that same place and observe each of those details that I have engraved in my memory. Fate must have acted for me because I would probably never have spoken to her. My shyness outweighed any desire. It was perhaps an embarrassing moment, but thanks to that moment I met her.

— Do you like that song? —she asked me the first time. I could barely speak, the most beautiful woman with the most attractive personality in the place was addressing me. So many things went through my mind, but above all a great emotion invaded my body from head to toe when I felt a little interest from her part.

With a nervous voice and her body almost touching mine, I could barely string together an answer:

—Yes, it fascinates me, it is my favorite group.

The very idea of matching her on musical tastes was a dream come true. I was excited by the possibility of being able to converse with her, as I had rarely done with a woman. Her gaze locked on me again.

—Of course, I like it, a lot, but you know, — she magically smiled at me and my heart was beating exaggeratedly, —excuse my daring, but my friends and I are celebrating my birthday. — And we love that music, but it is like cutting your wrists, to listen to when you are nostalgic.

From me nervousness to converse with her, I had moved on to feel ashamed, even as she tried to be subtle in the following comment:

— Do not be offended, but it is a special date, and we would like to hear something different. The waiter told me that you programmed all the songs, so my proposal is that you do us the enormous favor of canceling them. We give you the money you paid and let us choose some more festive music, please, and I promise you we will not bother you again.

She smiled at me Machiavellian, forcing me to send a signal to the waiter to change music, and with shame I said:

—Sure, it is your birthday, put on whatever music you want. —

I immediately turned my back on her and faced the bar, eager to continue drinking.

— How many songs did you pay for on the jukebox? — she replied putting her hand on my back to make me turn around.

— Forget it, it is your birthday, take it as one more gift.

And I did not know what else to say. I was intimidated by the look of her.

—Thank you very much, you have brightened my night, — she expressed to make me feel good and then she let out one more smile to at least leave me happy to have met her, even if it was in an embarrassing situation.

—Nice to meet you, I hope we meet again another day. —

Obviously, she said that out of elementary courtesy because she did not even know my name, nor did I know hers, and she would not ask me, not even me. Not because she did not want to, but because my nerves about having her close silenced me.

That was a rough start to our romantic story together.

Fifteen years later, our relationship was different, I was no longer a stranger to her. On the contrary, we knew each other too much, even without knowing how long her first marriage had lasted and how long she had been from the second, she could assure that she had made love to me more times than to someone else in her life. Sometimes she even tormented me and at other times I de—

stressed doing those accounts, estimating how many times each of my successors could have been with her. Because, furthermore, the first man in her life had been me. It was a fact that no one could love her as much as I do.

That day, as always, she sat right in front of me, leaving her sunglasses on the right side of the table, next to her car keys. Her gaze mesmerized me. We talk about trivial things to break the ice and feel more secure.

— What will you order? — I asked her. It was always me who took our orders wherever we went, although I was sure that she would order a cappuccino and a house bread.

—A cappuccino and homemade bread, please. — What will you ask for?

—A double espresso and a glass of water to hydrate myself. —

We deepened as the minutes passed and touched on more sensitive topics, such as pleasant memories of the city and the moments we lived together.

— Don't tell me you still remember when we met here fifteen years ago?

Her question offended me. She also remembered the date of our first kiss. The day we were together for the first time at her house, practically all the important dates.

— Do you wish I did not remember? You behaved super arrogant — I replied jokingly, and she blushed.

— Isn't it true, that is, how could you listen to that music? You wanted us to do a collective suicide in the cafeteria, to take our knives from the table and cut our veins? —Her jokes on me were witty and I was pleased to see her with her mocking smile—besides, do not even claim that on our first date here a few months later they almost had to graft me because of the burn you gave me with your hot espresso.

—I give up, do not shoot. I apologize for mentioning that. — I cut her off in her comments, and at the same time we burst out laughing.

Minutes later we delve into the complicated issues.

— And why didn't you get married? — was her first cyanide—marinated dart. I could have told her: —because I will never love anyone like you—, but I could not reveal my weapons before my time.

— Who was going to marry me?, I listen to depressing music, my clumsiness causes injuries to people with the hotness of my coffee, only you had mercy on me.

She was laughing like never before and she looked very beautiful. And yet she was a bit uncomfortable with the comment, which was unfair to me. We had been ourselves and now I could not bring up racy things because it made her uncomfortable. You were eating from my hand, I thought at the time.

— Better tell me, where did you meet your current husband? —

— Current? That sounds strange, but you are right, it is the current one — apparently my comments bothered her, but she had to endure. - I will be brief; he was the attorney who handled my divorce case.

Her confession made me so angry that I was about to throw a cruel joke that would have ended the meeting instantly. (—So, if you had been a widow, you would have married the funeral service salesman, — I told myself). It was a merciless comment, but it was crueler to know that this guy had been there, at the right time, while I was cowardly sheltered on the island. Better I decided to continue on the pleasant side of the meeting and only remember positive things.

—He must be an incredibly lucky man: having an alarm clock that drools him, — I blurted out.

—You're crazy: I do not drool anymore. Never say that again or he cut your head off with a spoon — she told me smiling and at the same time sad. And I, too, regained my mood and laughed non—stop. She had that gift of being able to change my days from cloudy to sunny.

When we were talking like two great old friends, I was able to ask her to listen to me for five minutes, without interrupting me. Forty—five minutes had already passed. She made time fly. We could just sit there all night and be immensely happy. We complemented each other so well that I still did not understand why one day we both decided to move away. On my part, it was the biggest stupidity, I admit it. Although I enjoyed being with her too much, I could not afford to put off my proposal, as I had no idea how much time I had on her. It might be our last date in life, but I had to take that risk. It was all or nothing in an instant. My original idea was to talk for about ten minutes and from there tell her what I had planned, but my nerves got the better of me and time continued its march.

It is like when you are going to jump into the void, the difficult thing is to take the step, but already being in the air nothing and nobody will be able to prevent it, that is why, although my body weighed me because of how nervous I was every time I tried to start I managed to raise my hand that I felt very heavy due to stress, as I had planned to start the difficult part of the reunion. That was the signal for the waiter to put on that music that relaxed me and to give instructions so that no one from the staff came to the table at that moment.

I took a fairly long, deep sip of my espresso and looked into her eyes.

—There is something I want to tell you, — I said with little breath in my lungs, and due to nervousness, I took another sip of my espresso to finish it, while turning around to verify that nothing interrupted that perfect moment, —but I want you to listen in detail every word I am going to say to you and analyze thoroughly without making any judgment. Just listen to me and do not interrupt me no matter how crazy and atrocious everything I am going to tell you sounds to you. Please, I ask you.

— You scare me! Count on it. I will listen to you attentively.

She got comfortable on the couch like a patient in her therapy with her psychoanalyst, she crossed her legs and drank a little of her cappuccino leaving that foam on her beautiful lips generating even more nervousness.

— Tell me what is so atrocious? — She returned to the attack.

Maybe I misused that word, but at that time I could not explain, I just had to tell her the reason for our appointment. I gulped and put all my concentration on that moment. Everything was moving in slow motion and the sunlight intensified in the window feeling more heat than usual, making me sweat as it combined with my stress.

—On more than one occasion you told me that I was the love of your life, — I reminded her, and her pupils dilated a little. I took a large drink from the glass of water on the table. The nerves choked me, and I could barely spin each word until I was little by little feeling like I was getting rid of that weight that prevented me from expressing myself. - And in equal or greater number of times I answered you, without hesitation, that you were also one for me. You may think there is no point in remembering the past, but it is indelible and unalterable, despite us or whoever it is. Just as you have not forgotten that in this very place we met that spring night when you bribed me to change music.

She gave a slight smile that gave me great confidence to continue. She reminded me of the need to do everything right to get that smile back with me again.

—And not all memories are pleasant, — I told her, —there are also too painful memories, like when I found out about your wedding, I felt that I had lost you forever. I was even there outside the church, in the distance, observing how you entered to fulfill that commitment and it was not with me; each step of yours was one more thrust in my chest. That is the only reason why you did not see me again, I fled to the island to not know more about you and to try to erase all traces, no matter how deep, of us. I know it is stupid and childish, but I decided to do so. I could not bear the pain of being in the same place and not being with you.

We both sighed deeply and took a breath to continue my story:

— One day I realized that I could not forget you no matter how much I ran away, and I decided to return. And what was my surprise? That you are more beautiful than ever and that you are married, but for the second time — she wiped with a napkin a few drops that began to emanate from her forehead. It was not the heat that made her sweat, it was my words when she reached that moment when she felt extremely uncomfortable, however, she endured listening until the end. It was the least she could do for me after she had emptied my life. I swallowed again so I could speak clearly and was not distracted by the immense desire I had to cry just to get to that part. - You cannot imagine how I felt: the stupidest man on the face of the Earth, for not having been there when you no longer had any commitment, while I was whining on my island trying to forget you. I was sad to think that your heart could not only forget me once, but twice. Full of rage for having lost every opportunity with you. Inconsolable because nothing could change destiny anymore. And I returned to my exile on the island, no longer to forget you because I had realized that I could not, but to get away and not suffer anymore to see you now with another person.

I had barely finished spouting my demons on her in that spiel, and she shed a tear and I tried to bring her a napkin, but she rejected me and preferred to take another. Her gesture was one of outrage at my words, but I had to say everything she felt, and she continued to listen firmly. Her face reddened a little. It was to be expected, the things I claimed were not pleasant.

By that time, the sound of the cafeteria had already played the couple of songs prepared for that moment and there was music of all kinds, but she and I did not even pay attention to that, we exchanged glances at times and immediately we avoided each other for the pain of being sharing moments that appealed to our feelings. She tapped the black tablecloth with her index finger, nervous to hear me.

And I came back with a hammering voice:

—That's how I was sheltering on the island all that time, but a couple of weeks ago I realized, perhaps illusively, that the only way to one day have the slightest hope was to be close to you. —

—Look, — she said with a tone of quite annoyance, —I do not know what you want. Do you think that I am ...

I demanded her with another signal, notoriously hardening my face, to be silent and with my voice on the verge of cutting I told her:

—You promised not to interrupt me, only that I ask of you, let me finish. I deserve it, if I was ever the love of your life, I undoubtedly deserve it. So, I speculated about a possible future with you and the only way was to be close; Perhaps my love for you made me think in the stupidest way to make an analogy that, just as you could have loved others after me, I could never be left for dead in your life. Then I knew that this is not over until it is over, that I will not stop loving you until I die, so my only hope lies in being here, in the city where we met and lived. And do not make me look like I am crazy. I am not, I will not press you for a single moment I will only wait anxiously for that minimum moment when you feel lonely or sad and I will be there for you; obviously, you will not bend in love for me, just for a day to come to me when you are homesick. That alone will make me close to you, so close to run a minute from where you are but respecting your relationship so much that you will not even realize I exist. How? I will just wait; I will be here for you when you decide. It may be today, tomorrow, next week, next year, in a decade, but never forget that here I will be waiting. I can be whatever you want: your friend to laugh together until we are fed up; your rival when you need someone to fight with and make you see your mistakes; your cloth of tears when you feel pain; your partner when you need to undertake any adventure; your inspiration when you need someone to motivate you by telling you how great you are; your wall where you take out the anger caused by any adverse circumstance; your confidant to hear your most twisted secrets; your lover when you need love without commitment or simply your husband when you decide that there is nothing more to live for than to be happy with me. You decide, you will not see me, but I will always be seconds away from you.

I tried to avoid her gaze, but there were her pupils staring into mine. So, I decided to face reality how cruel it was. My eyes penetrated the depths of her soul. The offended was me, the abandoned was me, the one who was alone and lost was me. I do not think she would have the courage to endure several more seconds, it would be somewhat uncomfortable for her in a public place and hers was her pride put to the test, however, she challenged me with her look. She remained stoic. She thus she was without blinking and the hands of the clock passed quickly and neither of them gave way to remove the aim of her weapon on the prey. She broke the silence after a couple of minutes.

Most readers will think that she got up from her place never to see us again; optimists will say that she cried with me and instantly she brought her lips to mine succumbing to my most sincere supplication and being happily ever after. Pessimists will think that she confessed to me that she loved her husband profusely; and the most extreme would portend even a pregnancy or a toxic relationship. Realists will imagine a long silence staring at us without expressing anything given the vast amount of positive and negative thoughts, resulting in an uncomfortable situation, but at the same time without a final decision, such as the probable analysis of each of the good and bad things lived together, but even more like letting time decide the destiny of each one. Not leaving a definitive answer at the moment but granting the opportunity to fight and continue living in the fight.

That was the universe of possibilities. What happened, regardless of whether I succeeded or not, is irrelevant. The important thing is that I tried and did not die without thinking about it. And I gave her, printed on corrugated paper, a poem written for her during my journey over the sea. Perhaps it could help her discern.

> **Even if I die.**
>
> And when the last ray of sunlight hits the ground
>
> I will continue to lurk,
>
> Not like a wild animal on its prey
>
> But as a faithful servant, waiting every moment,
>
> For the moment, I need to heal your wounds,
>
> To dry tears from your flushed cheeks.
>
> I will not give a single span, without rest, without respite.
>
> I will be there again and again, dealing sleepless nights,
>
> Waiting for a slight chance in front of your door
>
> Forcing the universe to return you to me,
>
> Forcing him to give me back your spring skin,

Your burning lips and your childish humor

And my routine will be to wait for you,

One day, one year, one decade, my whole life

I will be there, reminding you who I was.

Forcing your soul to feel me and your mind to think of me,

Until you go back to the same path

Where one day you were happy

And do not go back to another path by mistake,

That is not me, or anything that I do not offer you,

I will shovel at every step, at every moment,

No, I will not stop, even if I die.

www.ingramcontent.com/pod-product-compliance
Lightning Source LLC
Chambersburg PA
CBHW020349110726
47898CB00003B/1100